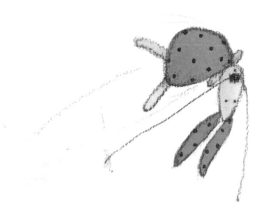

Copyright © 1997 by Michael Neugebauer Verlag AG, Gossau Zürich, Switzerland.
First published in Switzerland under the title *Ein Geschwisterchen für Pauli*.
English translation copyright © 1997 by North-South Books Inc.

First published in the United States, Canada, Great Britain, Australia, and New Zealand in 1997
by North-South Books, an imprint of Nord-Süd Verlag AG, Gossau Zürich, Switzerland.
Distributed in the United States by North-South Books Inc., New York.

Library of Congress Cataloging-in-Publication Data is available.
A CIP catalogue record for this book is available from The British Library.

ISBN 1-55858-731-4 (trade binding) 10 9 8 7 6 5 4 3 2 1
ISBN 1-55858-732-2 (library binding) 10 9 8 7 6 5 4 3 2 1
Printed in Belgium

For more information about our books, and the authors and artists
who create them, visit our web site: http://www.northsouth.com

Ask your bookseller for the other books in this series:
WHAT HAVE YOU DONE, DAVY?
WHERE HAVE YOU GONE, DAVY?

Will You Mind the Baby,
Davy?

Brigitte Weninger
Illustrated by Eve Tharlet

Translated by
Rosemary Lanning

A MICHAEL NEUGEBAUER BOOK
NORTH-SOUTH BOOKS / NEW YORK / LONDON

"Children, come and hear some good news!" called
  Mother Rabbit. "I'm going to have a baby."
"That's nice," said Dan.
"A what?" panted Donny, rushing in.
"A baby, a new baby," murmured Daisy dreamily.
"I thought *I* was your baby," muttered Davy.

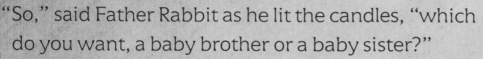

"So," said Father Rabbit as he lit the candles, "which
do you want, a baby brother or a baby sister?"
"Either is fine with me," said Dan.
"I'd like a brother," said Donny.
"No, a sister!" squeaked Daisy.
Davy said nothing at all.

That night, Daisy whispered: "When the baby comes, there will be seven of us—just like the seven dwarfs. Isn't it exciting?" Davy wasn't excited. He was wondering if he would still get second helpings of blueberries when there were seven mouths to feed. His best friend, Eddie, had a baby brother. Tomorrow he would ask him what it was like.

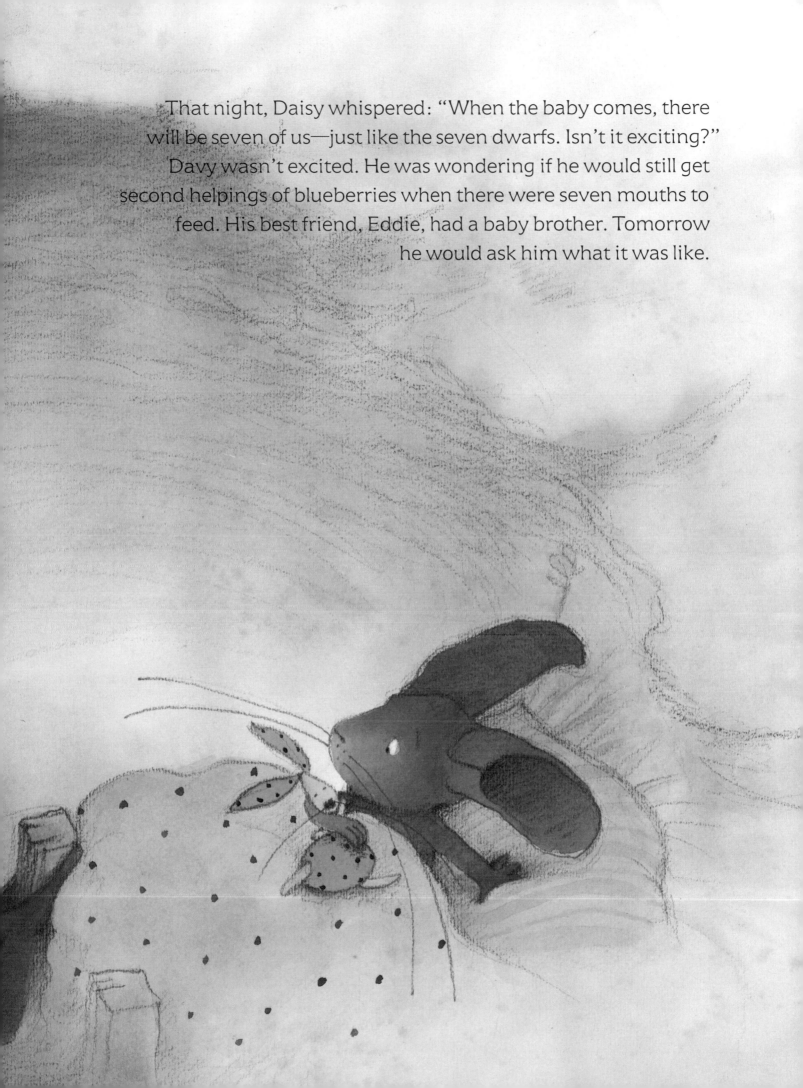

The next morning, Davy found Eddie sitting in the meadow.
"Guess what," said Davy. "We're having a baby too."
"Poor you," said Eddie.
"Why?" asked Davy.
Eddie thought for a moment.

Then he said, "Well, my baby brother is very small and weak, and he cries when everyone else wants to sleep. And he eats a lot. He keeps my mother busy all the time."

"Oh dear," sighed Davy. "Would a baby sister be any better?"
"Can you choose?" asked Eddie doubtfully.

"I think so," said Davy. "My father asked us which we wanted."
"Well, if you can choose, why not ask your mother for something
completely different?"
"Good idea," said Davy. "Thanks, Eddie."

Davy ran to his mother. "Father asked if we wanted a baby brother or a baby sister," he said. "But I don't want either. I want a pet mouse, please."

His mother smiled. "Your father was joking," she said. "You can't really choose. The baby is already growing here." She laid Davy's paw gently on her rounded stomach. "Soon it will be born," she went on, "and then we will know if it's a baby brother or a baby sister. Try to love it either way."

"I will," said Davy quietly, but he wasn't sure he meant it.

A few days later, when the Rabbit children came back to the
burrow, their mother called, "Come and meet your baby sister!"
"Aaah, isn't she beautiful," sighed Daisy.
"Cute," said Dan and Donny.
But Davy said, "Is she all right? She looks so floppy, and her eyes
haven't opened and she has no fur."

Mother laughed. "All baby rabbits are like that, Davy. You looked
just the same." She wrapped the baby in Davy's blue blanket and
passed her to Father Rabbit. "Please take the baby into the other
room and let me sleep. I'm very tired."

As soon as they
left the bedroom,
the baby started to cry.

"There, there," said
Father Rabbit soothingly.
He rocked the baby gently
in his arms. But she
didn't stop crying.

"Coochee-coo," said Dan,
patting the baby's bottom.
But she went on crying.

"Swing high, swing low," said Donny,
  swinging the baby up and down.
  But she still cried.

"Hushabye, baby," sang Daisy,
  walking up and down.
  But the baby wouldn't hush.

"*You* hold her," said Daisy,
  dumping the baby in Davy's arms.
  "No, no, I can't" he protested.
  But the baby rested her tiny head
  on Davy's shoulder and fell fast asleep.

"Well done, Davy," said Father Rabbit. Then he put his finger to his lips and everyone tiptoed away.

All Davy could do was sit still and hold his baby sister close. He watched her tiny whiskers tremble. Her ears were soft and downy, and almost transparent. She smelled of warm milk and fresh berries. Davy could even feel her little heart beating. He sat and gazed at her. She was so tiny. She needs someone big and strong like me to look after her, he thought.

Davy heard his mother calling for the baby.

"Here she is," he said, and carried his little sister over to Mother's bed. "If she cries again, just call me," he said.

"Thank you, Davy," said his mother. "You are such a help to me."

Davy ran to the meadow and danced around, laughing and
singing to himself.

"What's got into you?" said Eddie.

"I have a baby sister!"

"Oh dear," said Eddie. "Does she cry a lot?"

"Not when *I* hold her!"

"You're kidding," said Eddie. "What do you know about babies?"

"A lot more than you do!" said Davy, and the two of them tumbled
over the meadow, laughing and wrestling until they were both
out of breath.

Then they lay back and looked at the clouds.

Davy said, "Eddie, do you think our babies will ever be as big and strong and clever as we are?"

"Maybe, but not for a long time yet."

"You and I can look after the little ones," said Davy, "and teach them all they need to know."

"Like what?" asked Eddie.

"Like how to take extra snacks without anyone noticing, and how to look cute so Mother won't scold you if she does catch you. How to make bark boats, and whistle with grass stems . . ."

"And all the best games!" said Eddie.

"Like tag," said Davy, jumping up. "You can't catch me!"
"Oh yes I can," said Eddie, chasing him across the meadow.